Runaway Pony

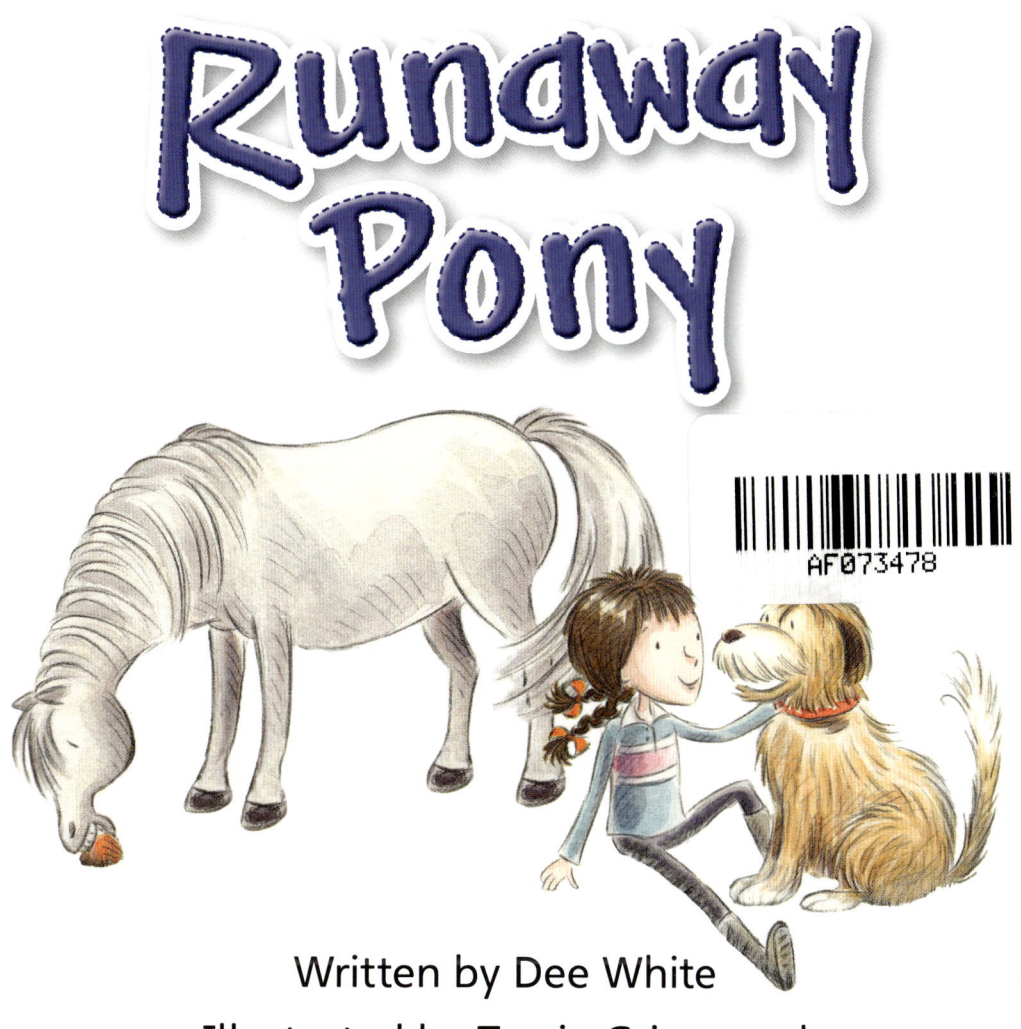

Written by Dee White
Illustrated by Tracie Grimwood

Pippa had lots of pets.

Pippa had a pony called Pat.
He liked to munch on apples.

Pippa had a dog.
He was called Spot.

Pippa and Spot went to see Pat.
"Woof!" said Spot.

Spot made Pat jump.
Pat got out of the pen
and ran off!

Spot ran after Pat.
Pippa ran after Spot.
Mum ran after Pippa.

Pat made a mess in Dot's garden.

"Stop, Pat!" said Pippa.
Pat did not stop!

Pat made a mess in Jen's garden.

"Stop, Pat!" said Pippa.
Pat did not stop!

Pat made a mess at the fair.
Buns went everywhere.

"Stop, Pat!" said Pippa.
Pat did not stop.
Spot got the buns. Yum, yum!

Spot and Pat ran into Ned's orchard.

There were lots of apples.
Pat stopped.

Pat got an apple.
Spot got an apple, too!

Runaway Pony

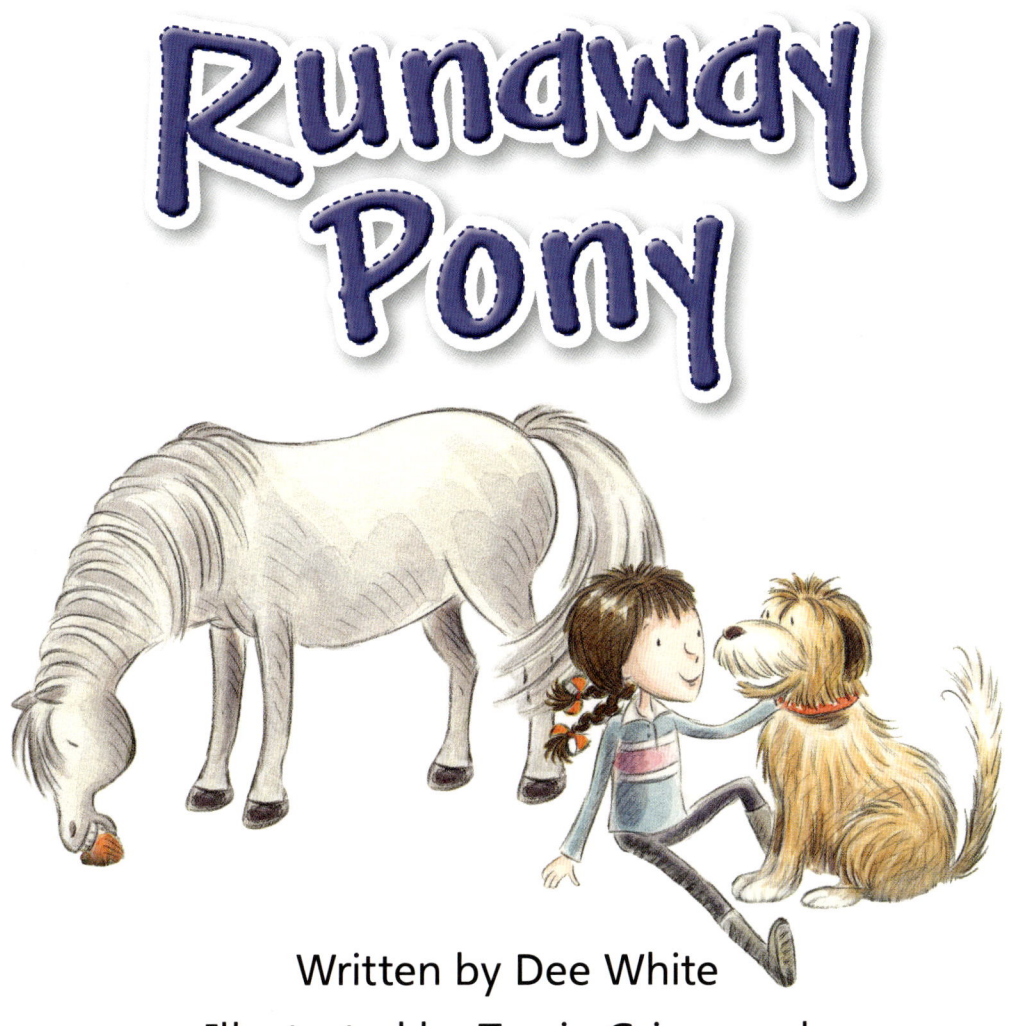

Written by Dee White
Illustrated by Tracie Grimwood

Pippa had lots of pets.

Pippa had a pony called Pat.
He liked to munch on apples.

Pippa had a dog.
He was called Spot.

Pippa and Spot went to see Pat.
"Woof!" said Spot.

Spot made Pat jump.
Pat got out of the pen
and ran off!

Spot ran after Pat.
Pippa ran after Spot.
Mum ran after Pippa.

Pat made a mess in Dot's garden.

"Stop, Pat!" said Pippa.
Pat did not stop!

Pat made a mess in Jen's garden.

"Stop, Pat!" said Pippa.
Pat did not stop!

Pat made a mess at the fair.
Buns went everywhere.

"Stop, Pat!" said Pippa.
Pat did not stop.
Spot got the buns. Yum, yum!

Spot and Pat ran into Ned's orchard.

There were lots of apples.
Pat stopped.

Pat got an apple.
Spot got an apple, too!

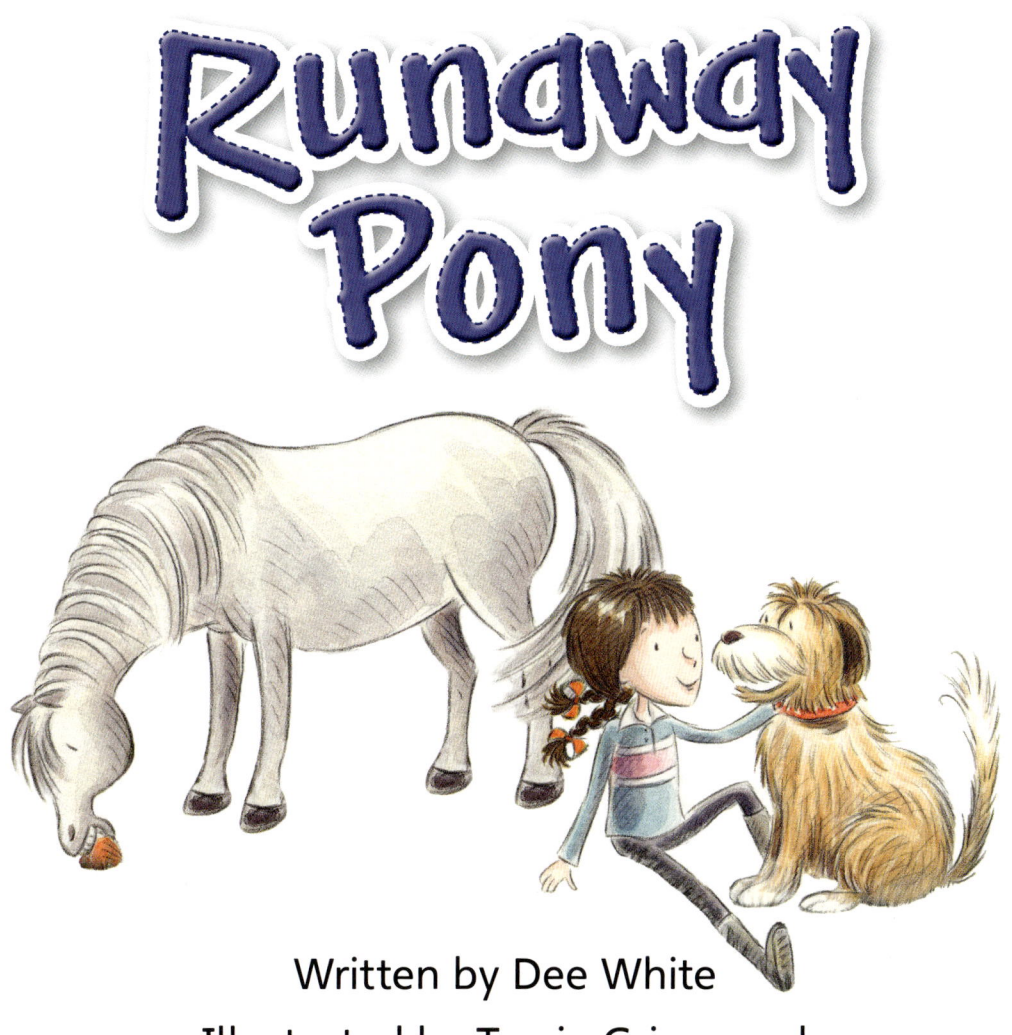

Runaway Pony

Written by Dee White

Illustrated by Tracie Grimwood

Pippa had lots of pets.

Pippa had a pony called Pat.
He liked to munch on apples.

Pippa had a dog.
He was called Spot.

Pippa and Spot went to see Pat.
"Woof!" said Spot.

Spot made Pat jump.
Pat got out of the pen
and ran off!

Spot ran after Pat.
Pippa ran after Spot.
Mum ran after Pippa.

Pat made a mess in Dot's garden.

"Stop, Pat!" said Pippa.
Pat did not stop!

Pat made a mess in Jen's garden.

"Stop, Pat!" said Pippa.
Pat did not stop!

Pat made a mess at the fair.
Buns went everywhere.

"Stop, Pat!" said Pippa.
Pat did not stop.
Spot got the buns. Yum, yum!

Spot and Pat ran into Ned's orchard.

There were lots of apples.
Pat stopped.

Pat got an apple.
Spot got an apple, too!

Runaway Pony

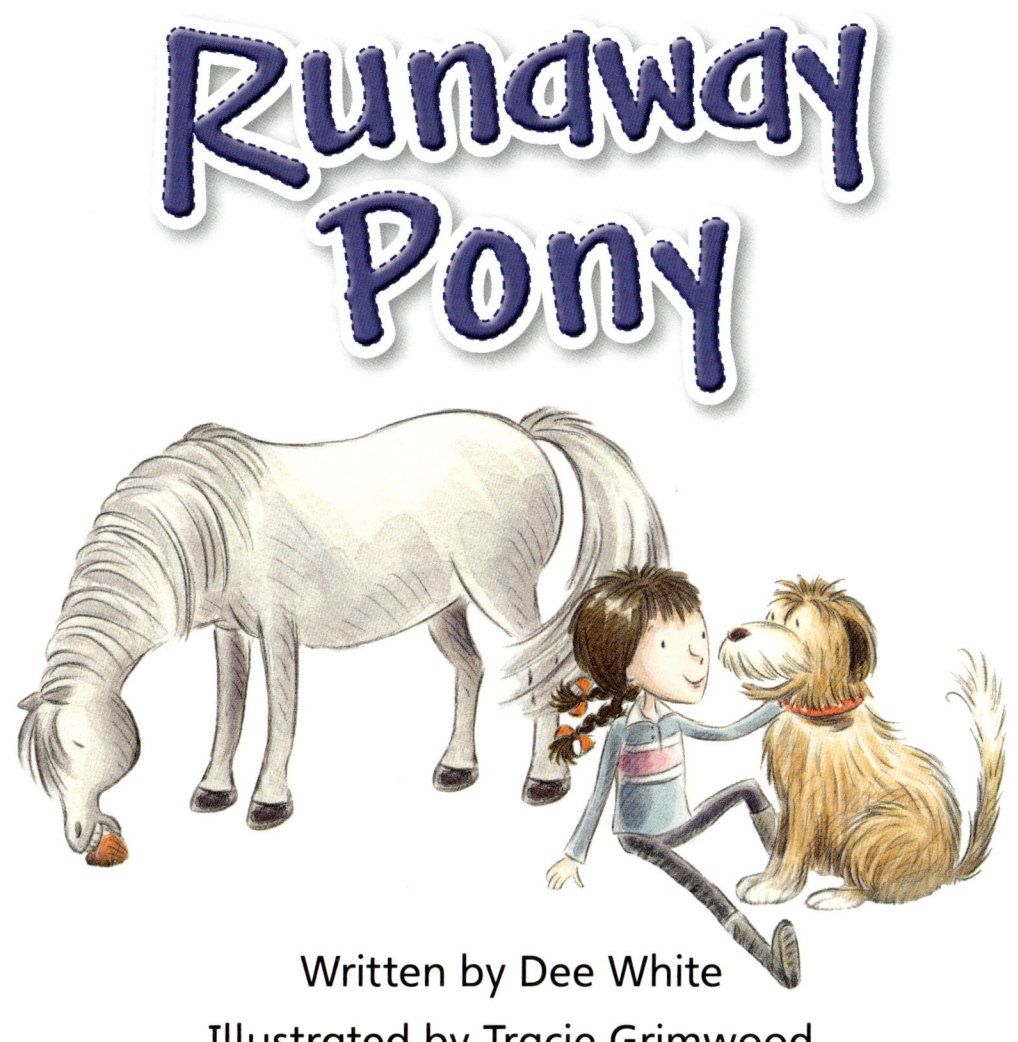

Written by Dee White
Illustrated by Tracie Grimwood

Pippa had lots of pets.

Pippa had a pony called Pat.
He liked to munch on apples.

Pippa had a dog.
He was called Spot.

Pippa and Spot went to see Pat.
"Woof!" said Spot.

Spot made Pat jump.
Pat got out of the pen
and ran off!

Spot ran after Pat.
Pippa ran after Spot.
Mum ran after Pippa.

Pat made a mess in Dot's garden.

"Stop, Pat!" said Pippa.
Pat did not stop!

Pat made a mess in Jen's garden.

"Stop, Pat!" said Pippa.
Pat did not stop!

Pat made a mess at the fair.
Buns went everywhere.

"Stop, Pat!" said Pippa.
Pat did not stop.
Spot got the buns. Yum, yum!

Spot and Pat ran into Ned's orchard.

There were lots of apples.
Pat stopped.

Pat got an apple.
Spot got an apple, too!

Runaway Pony

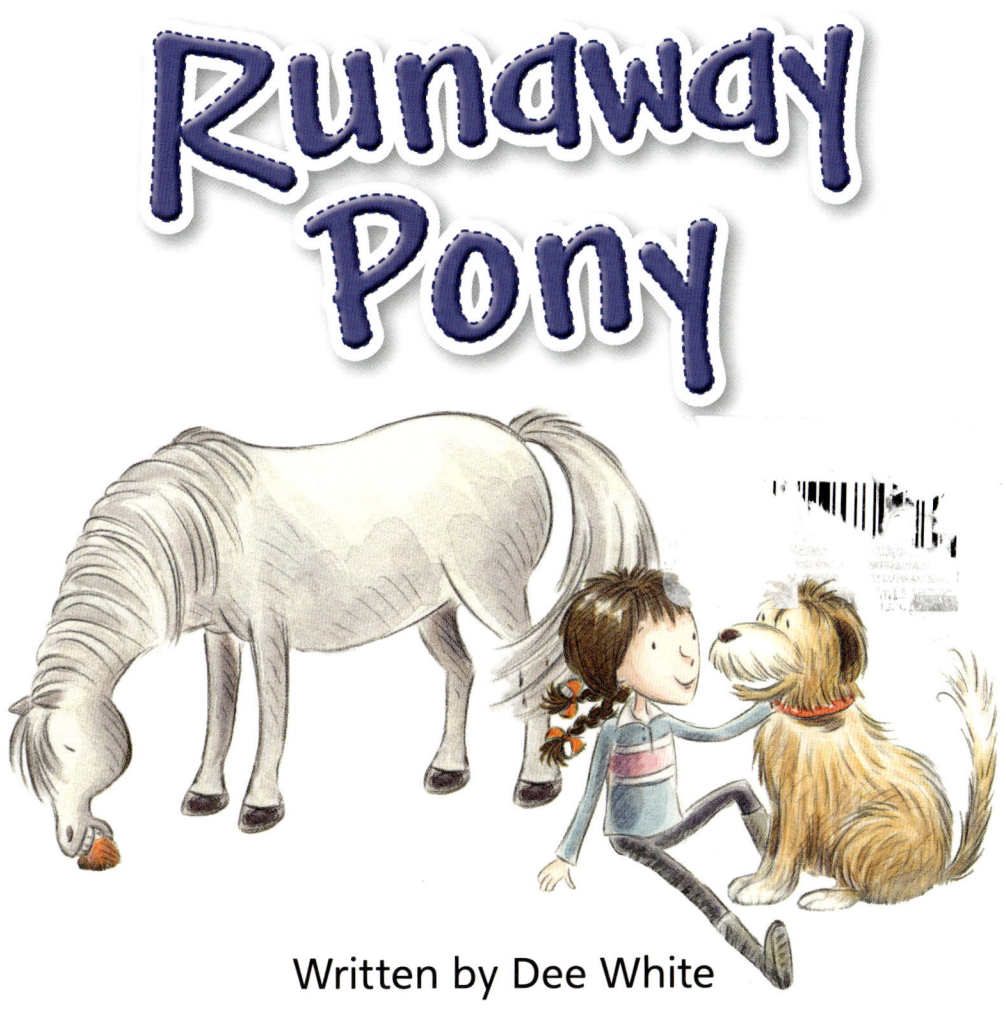

Written by Dee White
Illustrated by Tracie Grimwood

Pippa had lots of pets.

Pippa had a pony called Pat.
He liked to munch on apples.

Pippa had a dog.
He was called Spot.

Pippa and Spot went to see Pat.
"Woof!" said Spot.

Spot made Pat jump.
Pat got out of the pen
and ran off!

Spot ran after Pat.
Pippa ran after Spot.
Mum ran after Pippa.

Pat made a mess in Dot's garden.

"Stop, Pat!" said Pippa.
Pat did not stop!

Pat made a mess in Jen's garden.

"Stop, Pat!" said Pippa.
Pat did not stop!

Pat made a mess at the fair.
Buns went everywhere.

"Stop, Pat!" said Pippa.
Pat did not stop.
Spot got the buns. Yum, yum!

Spot and Pat ran into Ned's orchard.

There were lots of apples.
Pat stopped.

Pat got an apple.
Spot got an apple, too!

Runaway Pony

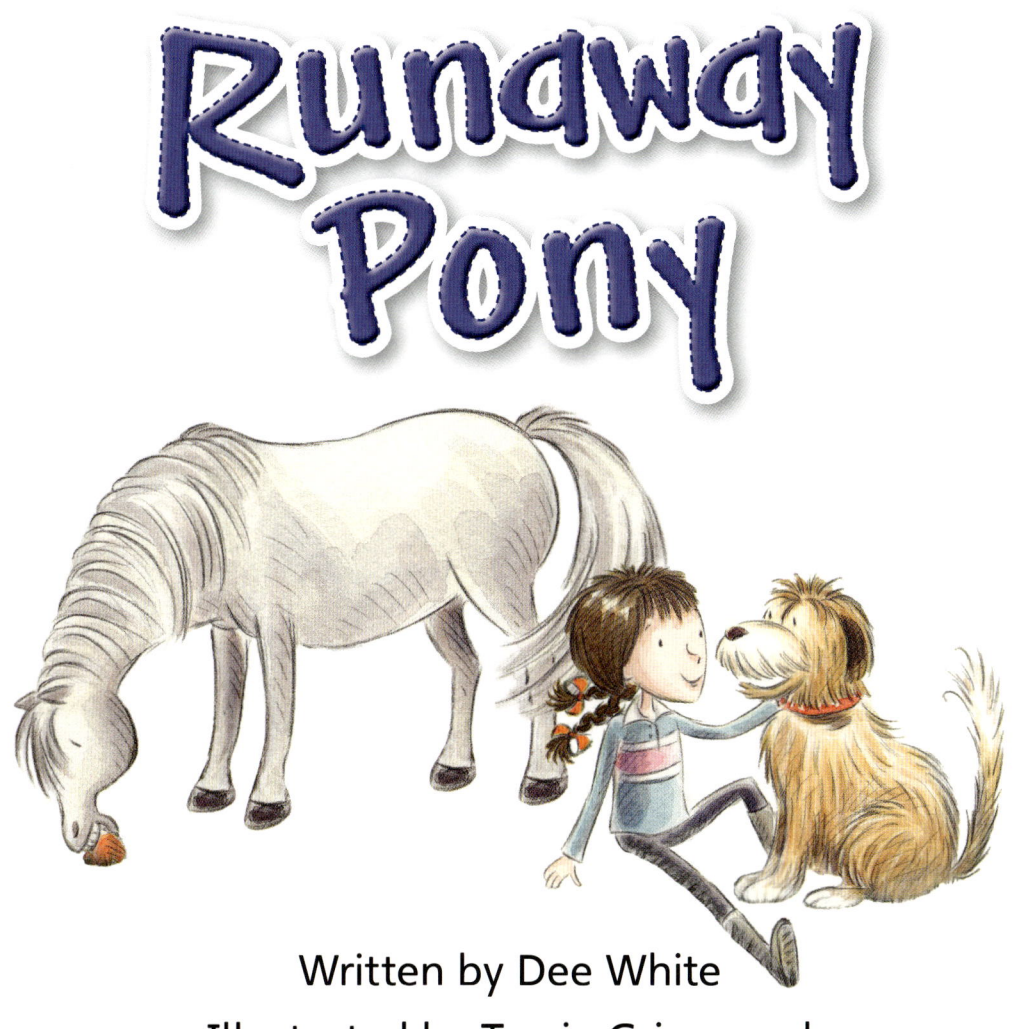

Written by Dee White
Illustrated by Tracie Grimwood

Pippa had lots of pets.

Pippa had a pony called Pat.
He liked to munch on apples.

Pippa had a dog.
He was called Spot.

Pippa and Spot went to see Pat.
"Woof!" said Spot.

Spot made Pat jump.
Pat got out of the pen
and ran off!

Spot ran after Pat.
Pippa ran after Spot.
Mum ran after Pippa.

Pat made a mess in Dot's garden.

"Stop, Pat!" said Pippa.
Pat did not stop!

Pat made a mess in Jen's garden.

"Stop, Pat!" said Pippa.
Pat did not stop!

"Stop, Pat!" said Pippa.
Pat did not stop.
Spot got the buns. Yum, yum!

Spot and Pat ran into Ned's orchard.

There were lots of apples.
Pat stopped.

Pat got an apple.
Spot got an apple, too!